SUPERFECUNDATION

MENKI ROJER

Hypocrisy is the homage that vice pays to virtue
Francois de la Rochefoulcauld.

Everyone knew Nildo Januh found himself in quite a judicial mess as a result of a serious incident in which he was involved with a Dutch "Makamba" schoolteacher. The Dutch schoolteacher, whose name was Pete Doorna, lived with his wife Nancy and their son Tom in a beautiful and impressive mansion in a high-class residential area called Girouette.

From the time Pete arrived in Curacao, he always seemed to be involved in certain businesses that had nothing to do with being a schoolteacher, which made him quite an affluent man over the years.

One Sunday morning as the Doornas were sitting in their home enjoying the freedom of the weekend, Nancy heard someone calling at the gate. When she went out to see who it was, she encountered a young boy wearing a cap and dressed in a red shirt and blue trousers. He identified himself as Nildo Januh. He asked Nancy if by chance she would have anything for him to do, such as chores, around the house. He suggested something like washing the car, cleaning the yard, running errands, or whatever needed to be done.

Nancy immediately felt a sense of pity for the boy, especially because of his decent and humble approach and the innocence that glowed from his face. Without hesitation, she allowed him to join the rest of the family on the veranda to enjoy some coffee and sandwiches. She said he could start to work after he had eaten. From that day on, Nildo could be found hanging around the home of Pete and Nancy Doorna.

The poor and humble boy, who originated from Banda 'bou, eventually became a full-time employee of the family. It had become customary for him to occupy himself keeping the yard clean, washing the car, running errands, and repairing whatever needed repairing. From the time Nildo found employment with the family, he was invited to travel along on vacations with them, no matter the destination. Nildo was a very serious employee who was well loved and trusted by the family.

As time passed, Nildo fell in love with Lisette Zunia, a stunningly beautiful black girl who also worked for the family of the Dutch schoolteacher.

Originally from Bonaire, she started working for the family after the elderly lady for whom she had previously worked was no longer able to pay her. Nildo's continual presence around the family's home as well as his way of behaving resulted in him also finding favor with Lisette. It even seemed as though Nancy herself was constantly encouraging them to get together. She always spoke so well to Nildo about Lisette: how she was such a good, nice, and extremely beautiful girl; how it would not be a bad idea if some day he would get involved with her and maybe even marry her.

As Nildo got to know Lisette better and they became very close friends, their relationship, at least from Nildo's point of view, was developing well. It even got so serious that Nancy allowed Nildo to stay over and spend the weekend with Lisette at her apartment on the family's estate.

However, Pete did not quite agree with his wife's handling of the situation. Tom, their son, also agreed with his dad on the issue. Finally, after many discussions and arguments, they both succumbed to Nancy's wishes and allowed Nildo to spend the weekends with Lisette. Both Pete and Tom were of the opinion that neither their home nor their yard should become a place of pleasure; that their employees ought to have some sense of respect.

Nancy insisted that she was in charge of the household and what she said went.

As a result of the continued in-fighting between the family members about the young man's love life, Nildo rarely spent weekends with Lisette.

Nildo could not understand why his weekend arrangements were causing such a fuss. He thought that maybe it was because Lisette sometimes seemed a bit embarrassed and uncomfortable whenever he stayed over for the weekend. Lisette used to tell him she would notice Pete and Nancy looking strangely at her as she went to prepare coffee for them on Monday mornings. Pete even seemed to be making insinuative remarks to Nancy, who would be laughing. Even Tom, who used to make jokes with her, seemed to be watching her from head to toe in a somewhat angry way whenever he knew Nildo spent the night.

It was obvious to Nildo that Lisette felt uncomfortable with the fact that her employers, with the exception of Nancy, were aware of her "doing it" with her boyfriend on weekends. Nancy was the only one whose attitude towards her did not change. On the contrary, as soon as she and Lisette had a moment alone together, she would ask her how she spent the night, and wanted to know about all the juicy details. She wanted to know how Nildo performed in bed and even how many "rounds" he could go in a night. It seemed as though Nancy herself desired to sleep with Nildo, even if it was for just a little while.

Lisette would always laugh as she bowed her head, but never said more than she felt comfortable to tell. She was not used to talking so openly about sexual and lovemaking matters. No matter how close she and Nancy were with each other, their difference in age made Lisette have certain reservations when Nancy would ask her about intimate matters in such a direct manner. Nancy told her on more than one occasion that she wished to be young again and as beautiful as her. It would take two hearses to drag her out of that apartment, she often said, after having some good love-making with her man.

"What call do I have being with a man as young and strong as Nildo?" Nancy would sometimes say during her conversations with Lisette. "Nothing would have stopped me from breaking my backbone taking him, even if it was meant to kill me." Never before, or at least from the time that she started to work for this family, had Lisette had a friend that would visit her or go out with her. She always seemed to be a quiet, meek, and reserved young woman.

At the end of the week when Lisette was off work, she always stayed home and did her usual chores. If she had to go out, be it to visit a friend or go to church, someone from the Doorna family would always take her. They used to take her and bring her home afterwards. Lisette's relationship with Nancy had become similar to the relationship between close friends, with one being too liberal and a little dissolute. They got along well with each other and Lisette enjoyed this very much, even though it did not always seem that way, especially with Nancy bombarding her mind with all this talk about being with men.

Nancy once told Lisette of her youth and how she loved anything to do with drama, dance, or singing. She had a great affection and passion for art because she always dreamt of becoming a big star some day.

When she graduated from school, she also took different courses in the field of art. Her parents even decided to send her off to Spain for some years to learn more about art on an academic level.

The city where she stayed was so quaint and romantic that from the time she arrived she fell in love with everything that surrounded her.

While giggling she told Lisette: "I arrived in Spain yes, but instead of opening my textbooks as I was supposed to be doing, I was busier opening my legs." The Spanish men were driving me crazy. I returned to Holland after a good while without learning one single thing.

"I did not give a hoot because I was young and beautiful and my parents had plenty to throw around. I did as I pleased."

After Nancy returned from Spain, she met Pete in Amsterdam at a fancy fair. They lived together in Holland for some time. Nancy went back to Spain several times a year, sometimes even as much as ten times a year to meet with her friends and lovers. When she got pregnant, she and Pete decided to get married and move to the tropics as soon as their child was born. They had enough, and were tired of living in cold Holland.

They both enjoyed the people and the warm climate of the tropics, that is why, cost what it may, they wanted to move to the Caribbean.

Nancy was born on the island of Curacao to a Dutch couple. Her father was a wealthy and powerful executive whose company made business with various Latin American countries.

At the age of eight, Nancy's parents returned to Holland because her mother was not able to take the climate of the tropics any longer. She had developed a skin disease and could hardly bear the hot tropical sun.

Pete and Nancy arrived in Curacao and fell in love with the island.

They promised themselves they would never to leave such a beautiful place and that they would remain until 'death do them part'. Both Pete and Nancy felt extremely happy to have finally reached the paradise they always longed for. In the beginning, they moved and lived in different villages. Pete got a job at a school and also did other business while Nance occupied herself with their child and the home. After some years, they bought a very beautiful mansion in the residential area of Girouette, where the couple felt even more comfortable and at home.

Things took a downturn after Nancy, together with her son Tom, had to go to Bonaire for a few days as Tom was participating in a tennis tournament. Tom always enjoyed playing tennis and it was even said that for his relatively young age, he was considered a great tennis player. Over the years he had won several tournaments and went abroad regularly to represent the country. His parents supported him unconditionally in this. Many times he also used to encourage Lisette to learn to play tennis and within a short period, she advanced very well in the sport.

This time however, Pete declined to go along no matter how much Nancy and Tom implored and pleaded with him to watch his son Tom participate in this tournament. He claimed he had too much work to take care of.

He insisted that he could not leave his business to go and watch a boy hit a ball. Pete told his wife and son he needed time to be alone to organize and evaluate the numerous problems he was encountering in his business. The few days that Nancy and Tom would be gone, would give him the opportunity to regulate a number of business matters. He even suggested that Nancy give both Nildo and Lisette a few days off so he could have the entire house to himself. He did not want to be bothered by anyone.

To avoid further discussions and arguments with Pete, Nancy and Tom finally boarded their flight to Bonaire and left their stubborn loved one home alone. On the same day, Pete gave Nildo the day off. He told him that he and Lisette were not needed as Nancy was going to be away for a few days.

Nildo appreciated this, especially since he had procured a little job from an acquaintance of the family. He had planned to do this job on the weekends, when he was usually off from work. Now, it just so happened that he was unexpectedly free to do this job and earn that extra little money right away. Lisette told him she would be spending a few days with her friend Lorna and that if he needed her during the night, he would know where to find her.

Lusi Lombardo, Pete's next-door neighbor's housekeeper, heard a loud and hearty laughter coming from Pete's yard one morning while Nancy and Tom were still away. It seemed as though someone was tickling another person without ceasing. Also, because of the constant sound of splashing water, she knew that more than one person must have been swimming in Pete's pool.

The girl was well aware that on that particular day no one was supposed to be home. Nancy had asked her before she left to keep an eye on the house. She promised to do that for sure. Not only was Lusi eager to comply with Nancy's request, but she also wanted to satisfy her inquisitive mind. Lusi went to the kitchen and grabbed the mini-stepladder she used to clean the windows. She quietly placed it against the wall and climbed it to get a better view of her neighbor's yard. At first she thought the disturbance must have been caused by the young rascals who hung around the streets daily.

Whenever they thought no one was at home, they would come in groups and jump into the pool while one of them would stand guard outside in case someone came home. If they were there when Pete or Nancy came home, they would swiftly run away within the time the remote controlled gate would slowly open and close again. Their jumping into the pool had become such a habit that Pete had decided to allow them to swim as long as they did not take anything without his permission, or destroy anything in his garden.

To Lusi's greatest astonishment, she saw Pete and Lisette swimming in the pool, both as naked as the day they were born. When Lusi quietly shoved her head between a bunch of ivy leaves to avoid being noticed, she got the shock of her life when she saw how they passionately caressed each other, laughing and kissing all over each other's bodies.

Look at that worthless, disgraceful, good-for-nothing, she thought to herself. She became even more heated as she watched Pete and Lisette making love in the pool.

Lusi had good reason to look upon Pete with disgust. To her, Pete was a worthless sex abuser with so many dirty ways. When Lusi first arrived to work for Pete's neighbors, Pete often harassed her. He used to peep at her from between the openings of the walls, whistling at her and telling her all kinds of dirty things. She never encouraged Pete or his advances, but she never totally rejected them either. As time passed, she became a little friendlier towards Pete and they started talking regularly with each other. On Wednesday afternoons when Lusi got off work, Pete would leave the house exactly when Lusi walked to the bus stop just so that he could give her a ride.

From the minute Lusi got into his car, he would touch and fondle her until she stepped out. After long imploring and promising that he would do whatever she wanted and needed, Lusi gave in to Pete and complied with his desires.

As he beseeched her on his knees, she allowed him to feel and suck her breasts. Pete promised her one hundred dollars. They both agreed to meet at six thirty in the bushes behind the Suvek Ballpark, under the big tamarind tree. Pete always took a walk late in the afternoon to keep his body flexible, so no one would notice or suspect anything strange on that day.

Like a gluttonous puppy, Pete began sucking, pulling, and rubbing her breasts. He continued for a long while, even to the point where a loose front tooth fell out and stuck on one of Lusi's nipples. Her breasts became blue and were very sore and painful for over a week. After Pete had finished, he gave Lusi ten dollars and two packs of stale old Verkade biscuits. He told her she would get more money next time.

Lusi couldn't watch any more of the poolside lovemaking; she quietly moved away from the wall and went inside. Her face was flushed with fury as rage grew in her from seeing Pete in this passionate amorous fête with Lisette. At one point she even wanted to shout at them so they would know that she saw them; especially that worthless, good-for-nothing Pete. She decided to pick up the phone and call Nildo to bring this to his attention. She would explain the vulgarity and dirtiness she witnessed Pete doing with his girlfriend.

After the surprising phone call from Lusi, Nildo rushed to Pete's home to surprise the couple right in the middle of their amorous act. When he arrived, Lisette had her arms around Pete, kissing him in his neck, stuck to him in the water; her legs were crossed around half of Pete's waist. Laughing and enjoying herself, she kept asking: "Is it good Pete, do you like it Pete, is it sweet Pete?"

Nildo stood there looking for about a minute, which seemed to go on forever, as he heard and saw this dramatic scene taking place right before his eyes. Lisette suddenly looked up when she saw Nildo standing there. She began yelling hysterically without ceasing: "Mister Pete, Nildo. Mister Pete, Nildo." Without wasting any time, Pete jumped out of the water and started shouting at Nildo.

"Get out, you idiot. Get out."

Nildo didn't back down. He stooped down, picked up a cement brick that lay in a cluster of stones at the side of the barbecue grill, and violently threw it at Pete's hip.

Seriously wounded, Pete went down like ninepins.

Shocked by this, Lisette jumped out of the water and moved her naked body as fast as she could through the yard to her apartment. She slammed the door hard as if to tell Nildo not to even dare to come anywhere close to her.

When Nildo saw the blood on Pete, he got frightened by what he had done and he escaped as fast as he could.

The police arrested Nildo that same day. Pete was transported to a nearby clinic, accompanied by Lisette. He personally called Bonaire to inform Nancy of his version of what had taken place. Several police officers came by later that day to interrogate Pete about what had happened.

When Lisette was at the clinic before the police arrived, he told her to lie to the authorities and give them the same story as him. Pete lied both to the police and later to the judge, claiming that at no time had been naked in the pool with Lisette.

He claimed they were just taking a little swim in the pool, enjoying themselves, when Nildo arrived and started to behave very unruly and disrespectfully, creating a terrible scene.

He claimed that he told Nildo to stop making noise. Instead of listening, Nildo got furious, picked up a brick, and threw it violently at him, hitting him in his side. Consequently, according to Pete, he had to undergo four operations on his hip.

As Pete was a respected "Makamba," both the police and the judge believed his story. Nildo was sentenced to six months in jail, three of which were conditional, and he also received a further two years suspended.

Pete and Lisette told Nancy the same lies. They were convinced that Nancy really bought their story. Pete even suggested that they should have Nildo tested, to see if he had been using drugs on that day. He reasoned that they had never before seen Nildo behave in such an aggressive manner, being a boy who never was or acted disrespectfully to anyone.

Tom conveyed that a boy attending his school who knows Nildo very well had once told him that Nildo either used or sold drugs. They thought this odd as Nildo always had a lot of money and his eyes sometimes looked strange.

Meanwhile, Nildo maintained his silence in order not to involve Lusi in this problem. He couldn't tell anyone that it was she who had called him and made him aware of what was going on so that he could come and see for himself. He acted as though his appearance at the house on that fateful afternoon was nothing more than coincidence. Lusi also kept her own counsel to avoid any more confusion. She didn't want to get into trouble and lose her job, which would mean she'd get deported from the island.

Nancy and sometimes Pete often used to meet Lusi by the fence to tell her how things were going with the police, the judge, and also with Nildo. Lusi pretended this was all new to her and acted as if she never heard of anything like this before. All along, she was very concerned and afraid that Nildo would mention something about her being the one who called him to see what was going on. For that reason, she asked Nancy, Pete, and even Lisette about the developments in this case whenever she saw them.

When Lusi heard that the judge had sentenced Nildo to several months in prison, she was relieved.

If Nildo were to get himself involved with any other criminal offence during his two years of probation, he would have to return to prison and complete three months of conditional imprisonment.

Simple-minded, naïve, and pigheaded as he was, Nildo told the judge at the final stage when he was allowed to speak that he'd rather do his entire term in prison.

"If a man commits something wrong, a felony, then he should be punished for this," he said.

When the judge reminded Nildo that he alone made the decisions in court, Nildo replied that Pete would not stand a chance because he would go after him again when he is released from prison.

His sentence became unconditional.

Nildo spent his days in prison with much sadness; so much so that he stayed in total isolation without anyone even coming to visit him. He did not even have any close relatives who could visit him, which made his days of imprisonment even more painful. He spent days and nights weeping in his cell. He had loved Lisette very much, from the bottom of his heart. He always dreamt of the happiness that he would give Lisette and he had great plans for her, and yet she deceived him. Nildo would never have thought or believed that Lisette would have any kind of affair with Pete.

Lisette always used to tell him about Pete's mean and stingy ways as a person and how he sometimes had a nasty odor. She never mentioned anything about Pete ever touching her or disrespecting her. This affair had left Nildo completely broken and depressed. He loved Lisette very much, and every time he thought about it, his mind would revisit the vivid scene of Lisette and Pete in that damn pool. Alone in his cell, he wept bitterly for hours. The painful and bitter reality of his situation was that no one had told him about this, but his very own eyes had witnessed the entire disgraceful secret *rendez*vous of Pete and Lisette.

Shortly after he completed his prison term, Nildo met Lisette in Saliña. She had a huge tummy and was obviously pregnant. Lisette told him that Pete had left his wife many months before and that she and Pete were living a great life together in a super-luxurious apartment in the residential area of Mahaai. In a couple of weeks, they were expecting their first child. Lisette was wearing posh sunglasses that were pushed back on her head. She was clutching a large, exorbitant genuine leather bag and a bunch of keys in her hand. To show off even more, she opened her wallet so that Nildo could see her huge wad of cash and more than a dozen different credit cards. Nildo's world shattered when he stood there and listened to Lisette telling him what a wonderful life she was having. When Nildo asked her why she had done what she did to him, she simply replied: "I don't know, we'd better not talk anymore about that".

Despite all that had occurred, he always held on to the hope that someday Lisette would return to him, because he loved her with all his heart and soul.

Nildo's heart was gripped in pain when Lisette turned away and left. The pain grew even worse as she stepped into her car, the latest Mercedes model. She started the engine, honked the horn at him, and waved goodbye with just the last three fingers of her left hand, each finger seemingly bearing five precious diamonds. She winked her eye at him and then swiftly took off.

Nildo remained standing by the wall of a business establishment in Saliña long after Lisette had left. He was stunned and at the same time frustrated because he could not understand how the love of his life had suddenly taken such a strange and dramatic course.

He finally decided to catch a bus straight to Nancy's home to tell her exactly what had happened and why he had gotten himself in this trouble. When he got to Nancy's front door, Nildo rang the doorbell three times and, shortly after the door opened, Nancy appeared. She looked at Nildo from head to toe without saying a word, while Nildo was also in a state of shock. Shortly after, Nancy took a deep breath and asked: "Nildo, should I allow you in?"

"Madam Nancy, I came to offer you my apology for all that has happened. I have worked here for a long time and it was never my intention to cause any harm to anyone."

"Come on in," Nancy said.

Nancy walked with Nildo through the house to the back yard, where they took a seat by the pool.

"What wind drove you this way, Nildo?"

"Oh Madam, you really don't know why I decided to come and see you?"

"I won't know what your problem is if you don't tell me."

Nildo did not waste any time and immediately started to explain the circumstances that led to his arrest.

"I came here that day and found Mister Pete and Lisette swimming naked in that pool right there. For a while, I watched them from behind that wall, but they were so caught up in their lovemaking that they did not even notice me enter. I even struck my foot on the garbage bin, which fell down and made a lot of noise. No one told me, but my own eyes that someday will be eaten by worms, saw them in that pool.

"I could not remain calm any longer after seeing Lisette hugging Mister Pete and kissing him on the neck. Then she jumped out of the pool, exposing her nakedness. She jumped back into the pool and again embraced Mister Pete tightly while crossing her legs around his belly and moving back and forth, as though they were having sex. My eyes went dark and I could not control myself any more. Lisette looked up and saw me. Mister Pete got out of the water and started coming after me when I picked up a brick and threw it at him. It landed at his side, wounding him. Lisette started screaming when she saw me. Mister Pete was charging at me saying "get out, get out" when I hit him with the brick.

21

That is exactly what happened, not that story Lisette and Mister Pete told."

"Nildo, I don't believe that is the way it happened," said Nancy. "You could have killed the man or the brick could have struck Lisette in the head. You would have gotten yourself in bigger trouble".

"That is why I came to apologize to you, because I also believe I disrespected your home. Let me tell you something, Madam, no one can imagine what I felt at that moment.

"Did you know that I bumped into Lisette just a little while ago, in Saliña, and she's pregnant? She provoked and teased me even more and broke my heart when she told me that she and Mister Pete were living together and that they were going to have a baby. I decided to come and tell you exactly what happened so that you will not bear me ill-will."

"The housekeeper that works next door told me when I met her in Punda three days after I was released from prison that whenever you went out and no one was at home, Pete and Lisette would make love. They used to call me a henpecked little man behind my back; that is what Lusi told me. Then I understood why Lisette usually did not want me to stay with her on weekends, even though you had consented to this. Maybe all that time they were already having their affair without anyone knowing about it. She always told me that Mister Pete did not appreciate it when other men slept on his premises. I always thought that

Pete was just being bothersome, now I know he was just disturbed by the idea of me being with Lisette."

Nancy patiently sat and listened to Nildo, nodding her head from time to time to confirm that she was taking everything in. A little while later she said: "I always suspected that Pete was having an affair with Lisette? I never bothered my head with that because Pete always believed that he was making fool of me. However, I am the one who made a fool of him a long time ago. For instance, as far as I know, he believes that Tom is his son."

"What Madam? Whose son is Tom then?"

"Tom is Francisco's son. In Spain, he is called a Moro, which is an Arabian-like man of very dark skin and heavy strapping body, just like Pete's. He was a friend during one of my numerous vacation trips to Spain. When I went to Bonaire it was to meet Francisco and to introduce Tom to his father. To tell you the truth, I always had a feeling that Pete knew very well that Tom wasn't his son. At least, he must have had a strong suspicion. He is a worthless man and he doesn't even hide his face in shame. He loves money so much that if need be, he would even walk over a dead body to get it.

"Many times when we got into arguments he would mention that Tom had a Spanish appearance. However, it was only because I come from a rich family and have helped him to become a rich man that Pete tolerated me.

"Some months ago, I noticed Lisette's body was swollen and she could hardly eat anything. Any time she ate, the food would be spewed out, as nothing could stay in her stomach. So many times I told her to go to the doctor but she would always make some excuse not to go. One day, I personally put her in the car and drove her to the doctor.

"When I picked her back an hour later, she was nowhere around. She had disappeared. Pete did not want to make any effort to look for her either. That is when my suspicion got even stronger that something was wrong. He told me Lisette was old enough to decide for herself what she wants to do. He even said that only God knew what man Lisette had gone with at that time. Three weeks passed without us hearing anything from Lisette. Pete was constantly on his horses and he was very tense, while his attitude was becoming stranger day by day.

"Then one day, while I was sitting with Tom at the table in the house, Pete told us the truth. He said he was moving out the following day to go and live with Lisette because she was expecting his child. I got very angry and so did Tom, but I did appreciate his honesty. Pete and Tom almost got into a big fight. Tom called him a worthless cursed bastard, good-for-nothing pig. He picked up a chair to knock down his father, then ran into the kitchen and picked up a knife. I had to jump and stand between them in order to avoid it getting worst. A neighbor called the police because they were making a terrible din. Pete went out to the police laughing and told them that he was watching a ball game with his son, and they had had a couple of drinks. Tom told him he would never speak to him again. Tom called the man who for his entire life he had known as his father, a despised son of a bitch.

"Pete is more than thirty years older than the girl. I do not know why he wants to make a baby at this time. Must be for the child to call him grandfather instead of father. You know something, Nildo, a long time after he had left, I was still removing his things from a closet to throw them out. I did not want to have anything in this place that would remind me of him. In those days I still had a lot of anger in me but now it has subsided and I am not going to let my mind be bothered with thoughts of that man anymore. That is the way he is and he won't change ever again!

"I came across some receipts from a place called Begonia Inn in which he paid almost four grand. From the date I realized that, it was the same day that Lisette had left without returning.

"I believe Lisette must have called the worthless bastard after leaving the doctor's office, and he put up the girl until they found an apartment."

With a lot of grief in his heart, Nildo sat there listening to what Nancy was telling him. He never thought that with all the love he had for Lisette she would allow Pete, a dirty old philanderer, to seduce her, much less to go this far. What hurt him most was that Lisette had lied to him about loving him, and he had even made plans for them to get married and form a happy life together.

Nildo stood up and said: "Madam, I am leaving."

With an aching heart, his head down and his face all in tears, Nildo embraced Nancy, said goodbye and left the house.

"Don't forget to let me hear from you again, Nildo, see you soon."

Nancy had a lot of compassion for Nildo and she was deeply distressed by the situation in which he found himself. At the same time, she could not help him with anything but offering a few words of consolation. Personally, she had her own problems after Pete left.

On the other hand, Francisco promised her that he would leave his wife to come and live with her. From the last time they met, Francisco made many promises to Nancy. However, she never heard from him since.

Nildo left Nancy's confused, walking back and forth like a bird that lost its nest not knowing where to go. After wandering for a long while, pacing up and down, he got on a bus to Punda. When he got off the bus at the post office, he went to the Plaza and took a seat on a wooden box next to Fat Mommy, who immediately presented him with three lottery tickets.

"Sweetie, take these three tickets. Take them off my hands. The big draw will be tomorrow."

Downcast and without any taste for life, Nildo took out his wallet from his pants pocket and paid Fat Mommy for the tickets.

"Thanks honey. Now you know, what's good for the goose is good for the gander. If tomorrow, God willing, you win the grand prize, remember your Mommy".

As Nildo finished paying Mommy for the ticket, he raised his head and saw Pete passing in a car, driving slowly with Lisette sitting almost on his lap running her hand in Pete's hair and his half bald head.

Mommy, who sat there every day not missing even the slightest mosquito, took notice of Nildo's interest in the car.

"That black woman there with her doll face must be giving that Makamba a real good piece of ass that has the old man holding on to her like that."

Lisette's fingers cut through Pete's head like the chocolate and vanilla swirls ice cream Nildo used to buy down at the Portuguese.

Molly, who was sitting there also selling lottery tickets, was also observing the scene. She turned to Mommy and said: "Mommy, that is chocolate without milk, because chocolate with milk cannot be black like that."

"You ol' antiman you, you like too much mêlée, you yourself black; that is why they call you Black Molly," Mommy said.

"That's okay, I too have my white men that really like me a lot."

"For what do those white men like you so much, Molly?"

"Because I am tight, oooh so tight."

While the car was passing, Nildo felt his heart eating up inside.

"Mommy, you know, that lady there sitting in that car was once my girlfriend. I bumped into her one time today already."

"So, whatever happened that she had to leave you and go with that thing that looks like some scarecrow, my boy? You weren't doing your job well then, sweetie?"

"Yes, but I think it was about the money."

"That's true, now it seems like she's living well. But, do not despair my boy, what is yours one day must come back to you. What is not for you will never in your life be yours."

Nildo stayed there talking with Mommy for a while, then he left to attend to other business he had to take care of.

Later that afternoon, he had to go home to try to get some sleep so that he could go out to work for the night.

Back at the Plaza, the two lottery sellers were still considering the strange boy who had just spoken to them.

"Mommy, listen to me for a minute."

"What's up, Molly?"

"I was scrutinizing that guy standing here just now, until finally it came to me."

"How do you mean? Don't tell me he is also one of your lovers."

"You remember some time ago there was a rumor about a man who found a Makamba fooling around with his woman in a pool. He hit the Makamba with a brick and almost killed him?"

"I think I heard something like that, yes."

"Well, it was that young man who was standing here with us just now."

"What makes you so sure about that, Molly?"

"Because when I noticed him watching the car and then telling you that he was going around with that girl, right away I put my computer up here to work.

I remember that at the beginning of the year I saw that face leaving the courthouse. I hang out here in Punda the entire God given day, don't I? I remember that Makamba clearly, because he was limping."

"Molly, thank God it was your computer up there that started working and not the one behind, otherwise you would have been in trouble."

A couple of days after Nildo visited Nancy, she got in contact with him again and asked him to come back and start working for her again. Nildo took a few days to think about Nancy's proposition. After he had consulted some people he trusted, they recommended that he take up his old job. He could earn almost 300 dollars more working for Nancy than he was being paid at the place where he worked since leaving prison. Besides, every so often he had to work nights during the month and then during the day he couldn't get any sleep. His neighborhood was very noisy with racing cars, children playing football, and constant quarrels about loud radios. It was impossible for someone to lay down their head during the day and have a little rest. Considering all these things, Nancy's proposition was more than welcome for Nildo, who promised himself he would behave well so that Nancy could allow him to stay in Lisette's apartment and save money on the rent.

Working for Nancy again, doing his chores like he was accustomed to before, Nildo started to feel that in a short period of time he was becoming the former Nildo. Nancy helped him with everything that he needed and he was allowed to eat ever day at the house. Nancy even held Nildo's bank book for him. Many times during the week, Nancy would take Nildo with her in the car when she had chores to do around town. Sometimes Nancy did this on purpose as a close friend told her that Pete complained about always seeing Nancy and Nildo in the car.

In order to tease and harass Pete, she would drive around in the car all day with Nildo, sometimes even doing things unnecessarily.

The neighbors' housekeeper, Lusi, told Nancy one afternoon at the fence that a friend of hers who worked at the hospital told her she saw Pete sitting in the waiting room, trembling like a leaf on a tree. Huge drops of sweat were falling like cannon balls from his forehead when they told him Lisette had just delivered two babies. He was in the delivery room but could not handle it so they sent him out.

When the babies were born, Lisette was screaming down the place and making such a racket that the priest was even called in.

Nancy still felt a sense of joy when she learned that the babies were born well and that neither of them had any complications.

She immediately brought the news to Nildo, who didn't react and seemed to have mixed feelings.

After a while, he said: "Madam, I managed to forget about those people. I believe I have given my life a different dimension. I am taking classes at night. I am taking Bible classes, too. I do not want to have anything to do with those people because I believe they are villainous. I think it isn't worthwhile to even think about Lisette anymore. She is a woman obsessed by all those materialistic things. I bent over backwards to please that woman, but she was never satisfied."

Then Nildo heard the words he was longing for.

"Nildo, maybe it would be better if you stayed here with us. You can stay in Lisette's apartment. Tom and I will not have any problem with that. Soon Tom will be leaving for college abroad and I will have to stay here alone. At least I will have some company. Tom hardly stays home anyway since he got his driver's license. It would be nice to have some company around here."

Nildo could not help but smile as Nancy continued.

"By the way, have you noticed Tom around the yard since you have been here?"

"No Madam, he left a good while ago dressed in his gym clothes. I believe he went to the tennis court. He should be back any time now, because he told me early this morning that he has a date tonight at seven."

"I would like to know if Tom doesn't get tired of every minute this girl-and-girl- and-girl thing all the time?"

"Madam, what happened to Francisco?"

"I got in touch with him again the other day. He had been quite ill for some time, which is why I didn't hear from him in a while. Now he plans to come to Curacao to live with me because he has divorced his wife and everything is in the final stages now."

"Madam, do you love him?"

"I think so. He is much more romantic than Pete. With Pete, it was all about money. Instead of going to bed with me, Pete went to bed and woke up with my money."

"Someone told me the other day that Lisette is all about obeah now."

"Nildo, do you believe in all that hoodoo and voodoo craziness?"

"You may not believe, and you'll see it makes sense."

Nancy left and went inside after telling Nildo the news. Nildo continued to do his work and he noticed that Tom was home from training and that he was soaking wet.

"Tom, your mother asked me about you just a while ago."

"I don't have time. I must take a shower to go out. Didn't I tell you this morning that I have someone waiting for me?"

"See what your mother wants!"

"I'm going to my room first."

"It's your business, but remember what I told you."

"You work for me, Nildo, not the other way around."

Nancy was in the study when Tom came home. She walked up to his room and knocked on the door. But Tom had already gone into the bathroom and didn't hear Nancy knocking on the door. He was singing and whistling very loudly in the bathroom.

"Tom, open the door for me."

"Mom, I have to go out now."

"Where are you going, didn't you just get home? Your dinner is ready. I cooked for you and Nildo."

"Mom, Nildo has to eat at his own place and not at the table with us."

"Tom, stop that. I don't want anybody to be discriminated against in this house."

"I am going out with the Hindu girl around the corner."

"Oh, that's nice, remember to behave yourself."

"Yes."

"Tom listen. I heard that your father and Lisette got twins."

"Mom, that bastard is not my father."

"Tom, don't talk like that. No matter what he has done, he raised you and you cannot say that he was a bad father to you."

"Yes, but he left you for your maid, that is why I hate him. And on top of that, an ugly woman, a stinking black whore."

"Come on, Lisette is far from ugly. She is an exceptionally beautiful woman."

"Yes, but she is black."

"I always thought you both got along quite well. You both were always making jokes with each other, and you even used to practice tennis with her, didn't you?"

"That's true, but I don't want to have anything to do with that black slut anymore. Would you like to have a couple of black rag dolls as grandchildren?"

"Tom, I believe you are going too far. In any case, I will be calling Pete to congratulate him because children are a blessing. And besides that, I am not on bad terms with any of them."

"Well, I am. I don't want to have anything to do with those two dirty pigs, nor with Pete nor with that stinking whore".

"But Tom, be a little humane here, Pete's two children are your siblings, maybe not biologically, but legally."

"I am a human being, not an ape, so I could never have apes as my brothers and sisters."

"You are just like, Pete; you have a bad spirit."

"I bet."

Nancy left while Tom finished dressing. Like a mad man, he rushed out of the house and off to meet his latest girlfriend.

"Hello . . . Pete, it's me, Nancy."

"Hey girl, how are you?"

"Congratulations on the birth of your children; what are their names?"

"What are you saying, girl?"

"I said, congratulations on your new children, you finally managed it."

"What congratulations, girl? They are two monkeys."

"What are you saying, Pete? Nobody talks like that about children, and especially little innocent children; that isn't good, absolutely not."

"What innocent, what do you mean? They are two monkeys!"

"What are their names, Pete?"

"Yongo and Bongo, what else can I call them?"

"And what about Lisette, how is she doing?"

"You mean the Mother Monkey. She is still in hospital".

"Mother Monkey? You fathered children with her, Father Monkey!"

"Yes girl, that woman can get so vulgar."

"What do you mean, Pete?"

"I was by her side during the delivery and she was screaming down the place and saying all kinds of things. She said her slit was tearing apart, and her front was hurting and those types of things. I was so embarrassed."

"Well, of course, this is her first childbirth so she must have had a lot of pain".

"First child-birth, I don't think so, girl, they are yet to come".

"You are not going to stop abusing and talking absurdness about people, are you ?"

"That's the way I am, honest; you know that, don't you?"

"But Pete, are the babies alright?"

"Well yes, they are two monkeys, that's what I told you. I am very honest, girl, you know me. The little black one isn't so bad, even though it looks like a little devil's child. But the little red one is the devil himself, that is what you call ugly. Fugly!"

"If you lie down with dogs, you'll get up with fleas, Pete, just to use your own words."

"Yes girl, but I have my doubts. Pete isn't dumb, you know."

"What do you mean? Are you saying that Lisette has been playing away from home all this time while you were living together in Mahaai?"

"Of course. And it seems that she has been somewhere around the zoo. It is not too far away from here. Just take a look at our Tom, girl."

"Pete, you cannot compare those two things with each other. We have already talked about that several times."

"But still I cannot accept it. It is too much for me to handle. Tomorrow I am going to see the doctor to request a DNA test, because this is really too much."

"To tell you the truth, it's your own fault. You are too ungrateful; you want to be playing between young girls' legs, don't you? You love money too much."

"Yes, I know, he who won't listen to advice must suffer for it."

"Anyway, congratulate Lisette for me and tell her that I asked about her. And, can you let me know if there is anything you need when the babies are taken home?"

"No, we have everything. The nursery is completely furnished, and we even have a nurse from the post-natal care coming by."

"Well, since you have everything you need, I will at least buy a hand of bananas and a bag of peanuts to give Yongo and Bongo."

"Get out of here."

"Wait, wait, just a minute girl, don't hang up."

"What's the matter, Pete?"

"Can't we talk about it just once?"

"Talk about what?"

"About us."

"About us?

"Yes, of course."

"Now listen, I have my man and he is fine. You must be crazy. I think you have to be out of your mind. Gosh, you are so crazy, you know. That woman has made you half-stupid, you know; it is she who has made you like this. You haven't changed; you continue to have that stupid heat about you. No wonder they say that she worked some obeah on you, you foolish Makamba."

"Oh, you didn't waste any time getting another man? I did not expect that."

"Well, now you know. Goodbye."

"Goodbye, my sweet pea, thanks for calling."

"Jerk!"

Nancy's head was so exhausted after those few minutes talking to Pete. She hung up the phone to go out and call Nildo.

"Nildo," she called.

Nildo went to her from where he was in the garden.

"What can I do for you, Madam?'

"Nildo you know, I should have let you listen to Pete just now on the other phone at the bar next to the pool. I was constantly looking out to see if I couldn't get your attention to tell you to pick up that phone on the bar. You should have heard how badly Pete was talking on the phone about his two new-born babies.

"He even told me that he was going to have them tested to determine whose kids they were because they look like monkeys. He said that one is black and the other reddish and that the black one looked okay but the red one looked like a monster. According to Pete, it looks like the devil's child that was not completely developed yet. Beastly, very ugly! Oh my God, I cannot even remember now exactly which one he said looked like a piece of unformed devil."

"Madam, as far as I'm concerned, I don't have anything to do with that. One thing I know for sure is that Lisette's babies are not mine. Did you forget, I have been in prison for almost seven months? Prior to that, it was about five months since I was with Lisette. After that, she never wanted to, or never could, or wanted to wait until we got married, and all those stupid excuses. I am not the father.

"Very well, go ahead and continue your work"

Nancy became very curious when Pete told her how the babies were and what they looked like. However, at the same time, she could not verify the things Pete was telling her over the phone about the babies' appearance.

She always knew Pete to be an abusive man who enjoys making fun of people very underhandedly. Then he would laugh and talk to those same people whom he had ridiculed and insulted behind their backs. As long as he could see an opportunity to use them for his own interest, he would pretend to like them. He is a man who seems to be very sincere as long as it suits him. At the same time, he is the number one hypocrite wearing the emperor's crown of the Pharisees on his head. Pete was so downcast about the disturbed appearance of the two new-born infants, Yongo and Bongo, that he kept his word.

Without consulting Lisette, Pete went to the respective doctors and told them he wanted a DNA test to determine the father of both babies. The doctor, the psychologist and the social workers talked to Pete many times almost daily but he stood his ground. At his insistence, the necessary preparations were made to have the tests done in relation to Pete and the two children.

In the meanwhile, Lisette left the hospital and took her babies home. Pete gathered the courage and told Lisette that he had the DNA tests performed in hospital before the babies were released. This caused a big problem and a big row because Lisette realized that Pete did not trust her.

"So, is that the reason why they came and took the children away for such a long time, Pete?

"Sweetheart, it is not that I don't trust you, it is just that the babies look so strange."

"Are you calling my babies ugly?"

"Not directly, but . . . . You know, the results of the test could give me some peace in my bum".

"But you are the one who fathered them. Wasn't it you who told me that nature sometimes could be quite obstinate? Why are you calling our babies ugly now?"

"Yes, yes, yes, we will soon find that out, my love."

It was almost two weeks later when the doctors summoned Pete to tell him about the results of the test. Early that morning, Pete arrived at the office of the doctor in charge to hear the results. He was the first one to arrive that morning and for that reason, the nurse allowed him to go in right away. Somewhat nervous and a bit frightened, sat in front of the doctor.

"I won't beat around the bush with this."

"What is the result, doctor?"

"Well, Bongo is 99.9% yours, but the other one does not have the same DNA as you."

"How is it possible?"

"Well, it is exceptional but not impossible; it does happen in the medical world. We sometimes come across situations where a woman gets pregnant by two men. Therefore, what I am saying is that two different men inseminated this woman almost at the same time. Consequently, she carried and gave birth to two babies, twins, by two different fathers. In the case of triplets, or quadruplets, this is also theoretically possible. In medical terminology, we call this Bipaternal Superfecundation . . . ."

"Is it true that Bongo, despite his disturbing appearance, turned out to have a lighter color?"

"Yes, that is correct . . . . but doctor, that child is so my God"

"Well, you know, with the complexity of these so-called fraternal twins, what we call biovular twins, superfecundation starts.

"What is superfecundation?"

"It is simply extra fertilization or super fertilization. This means that the insemination of the female egg by the male sperm of more men occurs at different times within the same ovulation period. In the medical world, we believe that one out of every twelve sets of twins is superfecundated. This means that fertilization did not take place at the same time. In your case, I believe we will have to consider it a superfecundation bilateral, because in all probability there is another father involved. This is, in fact, not so unusual. Stories like this have even been seen in Greek Mythology.

The doctor could see that Pete was getting agitated.

"Would you like a glass of water?"

"Never mind, I'm leaving. In any case, thank you for the effort."

"Always at your service."

Pete was frustrated when he got up and left. He parked his car in front of a coffee shop along the main road, stepped out, and went inside to have two cups of coffee. Sitting there, he realized that whatever happens, he still would have to go home. When he left that morning, he did not tell Lisette he was going to get the results. That means that Lisette would not be expecting this bad news either. He decided he'd have to call Nancy to tell her what kind of trouble he had gotten himself into. Finally, he decided to head home.

When Pete arrived home, Lynette had already fed the two infants and put them to bed. He sat down in his rocking chair in the small porch at the back of the apartment, where he just sat staring in front of him. Lisette did not say much to him either, because they were a little vexed with each other. After a while he turned to Lisette and said: "Lisette, you really fooled me, you continued screwing that stupid Nildo. Yongo is his child and the doctor told me that Bongo most likely is my child, almost one hundred percent."

Lisette opened her two eyes wide and spoke with a commanding voice: "Stop talking bullshit. Something like that could never be possible, you stupid old jerk."

They started a big argument, cursing and slandering and throwing all of sorts of ugly words at each other. Totally confused and frustrated, Pete became upset and started yelling loudly: "I have to call somebody because I have to get this off my chest."

Then he picked up the phone in Lisette's presence and dialed Nancy's number to tell her the latest disturbing revelations.

Lisette began to kick and stamp her feet really hard, screaming and crying she swore to Pete that at the very beginning she only slept with Nildo two or three times. Since then never again. She had even got her period after that, meaning that what Pete was saying is impossible. She ran off to her room and slammed the door very hard, then she threw herself on her back upon her bed and stared at the ceiling.

When Pete called Nancy's house, it was Tom who answered the phone. When he told him who it was, Tom did not even give him a chance to continue talking and just slammed the phone in his ear.

Pete called again, insisting he had to speak to Nancy. Each time he called Tom would close slam the phone in his ear. The last time he called, Tom told him in a loud voice that if he continued calling and disturbing his mother's house, he would go after him and give him a beating.

Totally disgusted, Pete walked over to their bedroom door, knocking and begging Lisette to let him in.

"Lisette, please my love, open the door for me, no matter what, I still love you so much."

"Love you? Go away, I do not want to ever see you again, you stupid clown."

"Can't we talk?"

"We don't have anything to talk about."

"Lisette, I called Nancy several times, but Tom kept picking up the phone and closing it in my ear. Can you call for me and see if you can get Nancy on the phone?"

Lisette did not answer. Pete stood a short distance away from the door waiting for her to answer.

"Lisette, please do that for me."

"I told you to leave. I don't want to have anything to do with you anymore. You are a disgraceful man. Why don't you just go back to Nancy? You want to tell her everything, don't you?"

A sudden silence reigned over the house. Lying on her bed, Lisette wondered for a while what would be the best solution to this problem.

A bit distraught, yet in search of a solution, Lisette picked up the phone at the head of her bed and held it for a while on her belly. Then she rested it back down and again picked it up. She thought to herself, should I call or shouldn't I?

Call or not . . . then she dialed the numbers and called Nancy.

She had a very good relationship with Nancy before and after she had an affair with her husband. After Pete had left home, Nancy would sometimes bump into them and greet them without any remorse. Even the last time they met, Nancy told them that when her friend visits Curaçao, they could come over to visit.

The phone rang until it rang out. No one picked up the phone.

"Pete, no one is picking up the phone at Nancy's home."

"Keep trying, my dear, she is at home."

"How do you know that?"

"I just know."

"You don't know anything, I have been calling for ages but nobody is answering the phone."

"Just try one more time, sweetie."

"Don't call me sweetie!"

Lying on her bed, Lisette was thinking of calling her friend Lorna. She had informed Lorna before anyone else that she had something going on with Pete. However, from that day on, Lorna began distancing herself from Lisette and did not seek any contact with her as she did before. She is a girl that doesn't like any problems. Lorna was of the opinion that she had much too good a relationship with Nildo for Lisette to be doing this to him. Lisette had told her many times that she wasn't at all fond of either Pete or Nildo. Pete was a stuck-up old man, but she needed Pete's money. Whenever she undressed for Pete, he would empty his entire wallet for her, throwing out all the money. Sometimes even the electricity bills for Nancy's house would fall out on her bedroom floor. That was how struck and eager he was to have her.

As far as Nildo was concerned, he was just like a stupid fool. She only ended up fooling around with him a few times because Madam kept forcing her on him. At the end of the month, Nildo would give her all of his money to save for their wedding. Lorna had warned her several times to be careful; she shouldn't have those two men killing each other because of her.

She tried calling Nancy again and while the phone was ringing, Lisette's heart was rapidly pounding because she was thinking what she would say when Nancy picked up the phone. She thought to herself that despite everything, Nancy always cared for her and she would be willing to listen to her. Finally, someone picked up the phone.

"Hello . . . this is Tom."

"Tom, it's me, Lisette."

"Listen Lisette, that good-for-nothing bastard you are living with called here several times asking to talk to my mother. I told him if he called back one more time I would go over there and kick his ass. Neither me nor my mother wants to have anything to do with that stinking pig."

"Tom?"

"No Lisette, we don't want any part of that bastard."

"Tom, will you listen to me, please?"

"There is nothing to listen to, he is an asshole. Now he has you calling here to ask me to allow him to talk to my mother, who the hell are you, Lisette?"

"For the last time, will you lower your voice. Stop yelling obscenities at me and listen because I can't talk too loud."

"What is the problem, Lisette?"

"Tom, your father had them run a test on the babies to see if they were really his biological children."

"And?"

"Only one of them is his child—Bongo, the lighter one."

"You are nothing but a black whore, aren't you?

"Why are you calling me a whore, Tom?"

"Because you are a lying slut. You are a liar Lisette, you lied to everyone while you were screwing with him."

"With who, Tom?"

"That jackass Nildo, with his black prick. It seems like he still managed to get you pregnant, didn't he?"

"Tom, you know very well that it has been quite some time since I had sex with Nildo. From the time I started dating Nildo, we only did it two or three times—and it wasn't even anything to write home about. It was just to keep him on the leash."

"Whose child is that other one then?"

"Who was the one who used to jump on me all the time, before and after his father left?"

"Whaaaaaaat?"

"Tom, don't play stupid now. You are talking to that adorable little black princess whose honeycomb you couldn't stop licking."

Tom slammed down the telephone in Lisette's ear.

Lisette started yelling at him over the phone: "Tom, Tom, Tom."

Tom stopped talking, but yet Lisette had a feeling the phone remained open.

"Oh my goodness, now you cannot get away from this one. Carry on speaking, Lisette, I am still listening."

It was Nancy, who was following the whole conversation from another telephone.